Do Little Mermaids Wet Their Beds?

story by **Jeanne Willis**
with pictures by **Penelope Jossen**

Andersen Press
London

For Sylvie – J.W.
For all the little mermaids – P.J.

I knew a lovely little girl,
I think that she was four,
And yet she was as clever
As a five-year-old, or more!

She washed herself . . .

. . . and dressed herself,

And used a knife and fork,

She could dial a real telephone
And answer it and talk.

She could ride her brother's bicycle,

And write her name in pen.

And did she lose the pen lids?
No! She put them on again.

She'd given up her pushchair,
She preferred to walk instead,

But I hate to have to tell you this,
She always wet the bed.

She didn't mean to do it,
But no matter how she tried
There were stains on certain mattresses
And sheets hung up outside.

There were lots of soggy nighties,
And some matching underwear –
And guess what else went in the wash?
Her favourite teddybear!

She tried to give up bedtime drinks,
She visited the loo
On several occasions
But it didn't seem to do. . .

She found she couldn't go at all,
Not even for a sweet,
So she went to bed and worried
On a horrid plastic sheet.

But then one night, she had a dream
That, far away to sea,
She heard a little mermaid
Calling, "Come and play with me."

And so she packed a suitcase
With her most important things:
Her ballet shoes, tiara,
And a pair of fairy wings.

She found a piece of paper
And she wrote a little note,
"I've run away to sea," it said.
She fetched her hat and coat.

She found her rabbit slippers
And she put them
on her feet . . .

And dreamt she tiptoed down the stairs,
And skipped off down the street.

And did she meet the mermaid?
Yes, of course, I'm glad to say!
They rode upon a seahorse . . .

And some dolphins came to play.

They had a sing-song with some whales,
The oysters gave them pearls . . .

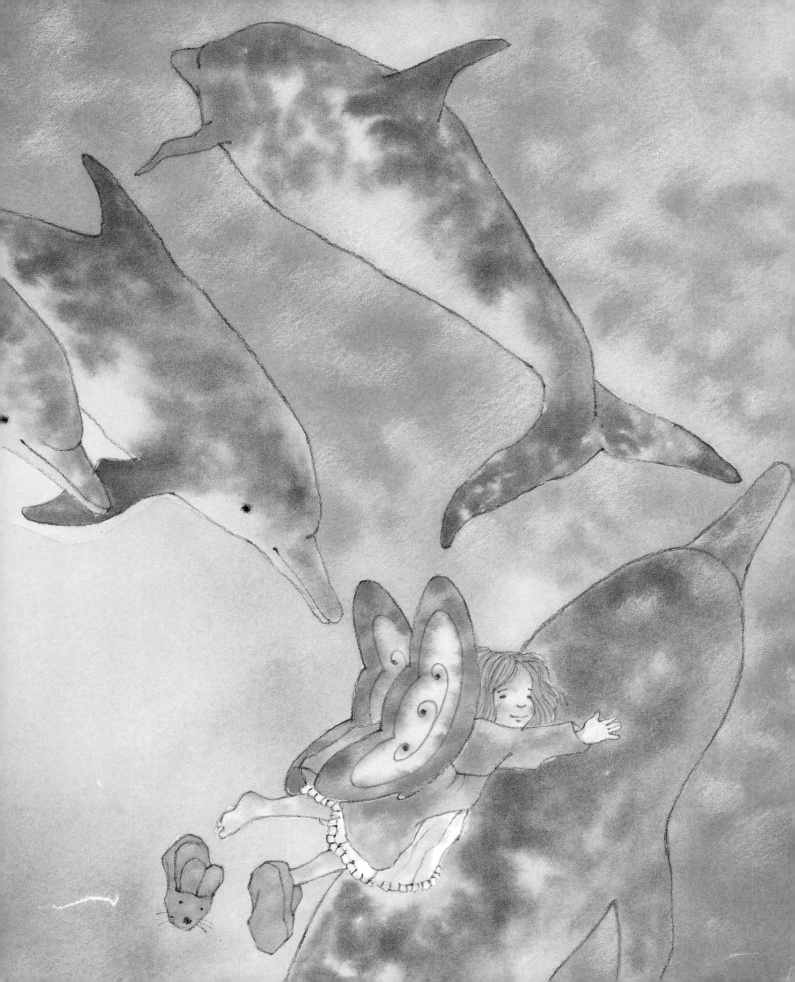

They danced 'til dawn with tiger prawns,
Such very tired girls.

They lay down on the seabed
On a mattress made of sand,
And our little girl was happy
For the mermaid held her hand.

And she said, "My bed is always wet,
It doesn't worry me!
What does a little puddle matter
In the mighty sea?"
She said, "You'll soon be home and dry,
'Til then, you're not alone.
I'm sure when she was four
The Queen of England wet her throne."

All in a dream they waved goodbye,

The little girl ran home . . .

And crept upstairs, her curls all wet,
Her slippers dripping foam.

She slid between her own, clean sheets,
And when the morning came . . .

She felt her mother kissing her
And calling out her name:

"Cecelia, your coat is soaked!
Your hat is wet! But why,
Cecelia! You clever girl . . .
Your bed is nice and dry!"

Text copyright © 2000 by Jeanne Willis. Illustrations copyright © 2000 by Penelope Jossen.
The rights of Jeanne Willis and Penelope Jossen to be identified as the author and illustrator of this work
have been asserted by them in accordance with the Copyright, Designs and Patents Act, 1988.

First published in Great Britain in 2000 by Andersen Press Ltd., 20 Vauxhall Bridge Road, London SW1V 2SA.
Published in Australia by Random House Australia Pty., 20 Alfred Street, Milsons Point, Sydney, NSW 2061.
All rights reserved. Colour separated in Italy by Fotoriproduzioni Grafiche, Verona.
Printed and bound in Italy by Grafiche AZ, Verona.

10   9   8   7   6   5   4   3   2   1

British Library Cataloguing in Publication Data available.

ISBN 0 86264 974 9

This book has been printed on acid-free paper